D1308388

To Ben

One Big hug

*Love
Grammy
9-25-2009*

Shirley Hillard

 A Mamoo House Book

Granny said to Matthew,
"I love you so much."

"How much?"
said Matthew.

"I love you as much
as one big hug."

"More,"
said Matthew.

"I love you as much as

2 bugs

in a rug."

"More," said Matthew.

"I love you as much as

4 doggies

standing on a flea."

"More," said Matthew.

"I love you as much as

7 elephants

climbing up a tree."

"More," said Matthew.

"I love you as much as

16 bears

wearing a yellow coat."

"More," said Matthew.

"I love you as much as

27 chickens

sitting on a goat."

"More," said Matthew.

"I love you as much as

49 frogs

swinging on a clock."

"More," said Matthew.

"I love you as much as

55 hippos

jumping over a rock."

"More," said Matthew.

"I love you as much as

67 crocodiles

singing out loud."

"More," said Matthew.

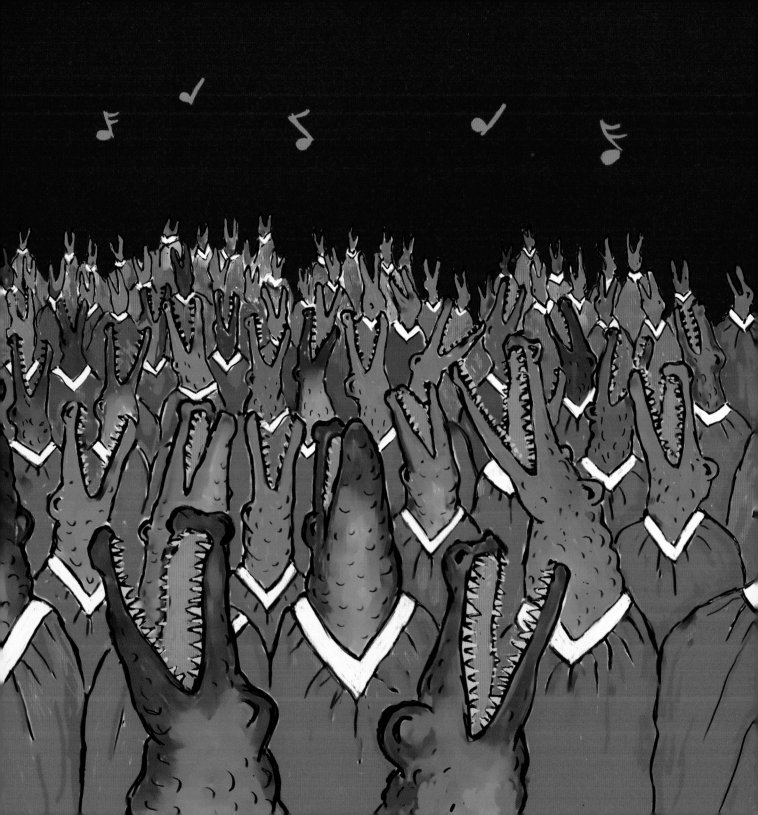

"I love you as much as

100 penguins

dancing on a cloud."

"That's enough," said Matthew.
"How much do you love me?"
said Granny.
Matthew counted on his fingers.

"I love you as much as

1 duck egg

floating in the sky."

"More" said Granny.

"I love you as much as

3 piggies

playing in a pie."

"More" said Granny.

"I love you as much as

5 giraffes

riding in a car."

"More" said Granny.

"I love you as much as

6 monkeys

hanging on a bar."

"More," said Granny.

"I love you as much as

10 polar bears

flying a kite."

"More," said Granny.

"I love you as much as a million stars shining at night."

"But do you love me as much as one big hug?" said Granny.

"Yes," said Matthew.

"That's enough," said Granny.

For my grandson, Matthew,
who taught me the game a
long time ago. Matthew is
very big now, but not too big
for a hug.

Text and illustrations © 2005 by Shirley Hillard

Mamoo House
1626 Wilcox Ave., Ste. 929
Los Angeles, CA 90028

Visit: www.mamoohouse.com

Publisher's Cataloging-in-Publication
Hillard, Shirley.
    One big hug / Shirley Hillard. -- Rev. ed.
    p. cm.
    SUMMARY: Is a grandmother's love for her grandson
bigger than a hug? Bigger than two bugs in a rug? Bigger
than the whole world?
    Audience: Ages 5-9.
    ISBN 1-933014-20-2

    1. Grandparent and child--Juvenile fiction.
[1. Grandmothers--Fiction. 2.Love--Fiction. 3. Family--
Fiction. 4. Stories in rhyme.]   I.Title

PZ8.3.H55237One 2005   [E]
                         QBI04-700507

Printed in Hong Kong

MAMOO
HOUSE

www.mamoohouse.com